The GOOSE That Laid the GOLDEN EGGS

Kathleen E. Bradley

Editorial Director
Dona Herweck Rice

Assistant Editor
Leslie Huber, M.A.

Editor-in-Chief
Sharon Coan, M.S.Ed.

Editorial Manager
Gisela Lee, M.A.

Creative Director
Lee Aucoin

Illustration Manager/Designer
Timothy J. Bradley

Illustrator
Agi Palinay

Publisher
Rachelle Cracchiolo, M.S.Ed.

Teacher Created Materials
5301 Oceanus Drive
Huntington Beach, CA 92649
http://www.tcmpub.com
ISBN 978-1-4333-0291-6
©2009 Teacher Created Materials, Inc.
Reprinted 2012

The Goose That Laid the Golden Eggs

Story Summary

It is time to pay taxes to the king, but all that Joseph and his mother have to offer him is a goose. They were told that the goose is magical and lays golden eggs. But they never see a single golden egg—until they give the goose to the king. In the king's luxury, the goose begins to lay the precious eggs. But the goose has many demands of the king. She must have everything she wants in order to keep laying golden eggs. The greedy king agrees.

Does the king pay too high a price? Will he be able to meet the needs of the goose? Or, will he learn that enough is enough? Read the story to find out.

Tips for Performing Reader's Theater

Adapted from Aaron Shepard

- Don't let your script hide your face. If you can't see the audience, your script is too high.

- Look up often when you speak. Don't just look at your script.

- Talk slowly, so the audience knows what you are saying.

- Talk loudly, so everyone can hear you.

- Talk with feelings. If the character is sad, let your voice be sad. If the character is surprised, let your voice be surprised.

- Stand up straight. Keep your hands and feet still.

- Remember that even when you are not talking, you are still your character.

- Narrator, be sure to give the characters enough time for their lines.

Tips for Performing
Reader's Theater *(cont.)*

- If the audience laughs, wait for them to stop before you speak again.

- If someone in the audience talks, don't pay attention.

- If someone walks into the room, don't pay attention.

- If you make a mistake, pretend it was right.

- If you drop something, try to leave it where it is until the audience is looking somewhere else.

- If a reader forgets to read his or her part, see if you can read the part instead, make something up, or just skip over it. Don't whisper to the reader!

- If a reader falls down during the performance, pretend it didn't happen.

The Goose That Laid the Golden Eggs

Characters

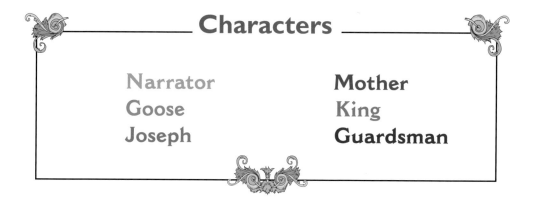

Narrator	Mother
Goose	King
Joseph	Guardsman

Setting

This reader's theater takes place in the palace of a rich and selfish king.

Act I

Narrator:	On the last day of the month, all peasants in the kingdom pay rent to the king.
King:	I've seen many peasants so far this morning. Are there more to come?
Guardsman:	Yes, Your Majesty, plenty more. You own all the land, so any peasant who lives here eagerly wishes to pay you.
King:	Yes, quite true. Isn't it wonderful that I have everything I could ever want?
Guardsman:	But Sire, don't you wish for more?
King:	I'm pleased with what I have.
Guardsman:	You deserve it all.
Narrator:	The king chuckles.

King: You are quite right. Well, let's get on with it!

Guardsman: Gatekeeper, send in the peasants.

Narrator: The king bites a turkey leg and then flings it back to the plate as the peasants file past.

Act 2

Narrator: Outside, a boy and his mother wait. The boy holds a goose that flaps and honks loudly.

Mother: Hush, you silly goose!

Joseph: Mama, I am frightened.

Goose: Honk!

Mother: I know, Joseph. But our rent is due. We must give this goose to the king. It will be all right.

Goose: Honk!

Joseph: The merchant told us that she's a magical goose. He said that if we treat her well, she'll lay golden eggs. Are you hoping that will make up for not having the rent?

Goose: Honk!

Mother: Well, yes, I am. Aren't golden eggs worth more than copper coins?

Goose: Honk!

Joseph: But the goose is *not* magical! I've done everything the merchant said. But no golden eggs! All she does is honk.

Goose: Honk!

Joseph: Oh, be quiet!

Mother: Don't worry, Joseph. All will be well.

Joseph: How can you be so sure?

Song: April Showers

Act 3

Narrator: Suddenly, the gates open wide. Joseph and his mother are called inside to the king.

Guardsman: Come and bow before your king.

Narrator: As they bow, the goose jumps down and begins to strut in front of the king!

Goose: Well, this is more my style!

Mother: My goodness!

Narrator: Surprised, the mother faints.

Goose: Fainting again? What a drama queen!

King: What is the meaning of this?

Goose: Your Majesty, if you only knew what I have endured with these peasants!

Guardsman: A goose that can speak?

Narrator: The goose jumps onto the banquet table. With her wings behind her back, she examines the finery.

Goose: Yes, I can get used to this. I'd like more silver and gold, though. You clearly need more of everything.

Narrator: The king tips his crown back on his head and rubs his eyelids.

King: Am I imagining this? Is this a trick?

Joseph: Sire, forgive us. We are as surprised as you to hear this goose speak.

Guardsman: How dare you! The king is the most rightly surprised in the kingdom!

King: Thank you, you are quite right.

Narrator: The goose interrupts.

Goose: Of course, castle or not, I won't think of living here without proper care.

Narrator: Joseph's mother steps forward.

Mother: My king, the merchant told us she is a magical goose. However, until now, she's been no different than any other.

Goose: No different? Do you compare me to simple farm geese? They are just cheaper-by-the-dozen-egg-layers. Watch this!

Narrator: The goose jumps onto the throne and lays a golden egg. It rolls into the king's lap.

King: Most pleasantly unusual!

Act 4

Joseph: Gold? How can this be?

Mother: Perhaps the goose is right. What if she can only lay golden eggs for a king?

King: That makes perfect sense.

Guardsman: What would peasants do with gold?

King: Precisely! And the goose is right. This castle needs a new wing. Three hundred rooms is simply too small.

Guardsman: Why stop at three hundred?

King: Well spoken, noble guardsman. Five hundred elegant rooms and halls shall be built instantly, if not sooner.

Goose: That's the ticket!

Narrator: The king's eyes widen as he strokes the golden egg. Then he frowns.

King: But wait, won't it take more than just one golden egg? Won't I need more eggs to get everything I desire?

Goose: The supply is endless.

King: And that's a grand thing indeed. So, if I want a hundred fine carriages . . .

Goose: You'll have them.

King: If I dream of a banquet with every fine food on silver platters . . .

Goose:	No problem.
King:	A magnificent castle . . .
Guardsman:	Sire, with a goose that can lay golden eggs, you will rule the world!
King:	Yes! I never realized I needed so much more than I already have!
Guardsman:	You deserve it all!
King:	I thought I was happy, but now I see there are many things I need!
Goose:	Yes, you'll have them all in good time.
Joseph:	What do you mean?
Goose:	The conditions for laying a golden egg must be just right.

King:	Guardsman, see to it that this goose gets whatever she needs.
Guardsman:	So you will get whatever you want!
King:	Precisely.
Goose:	First, I need full-time attendants. One of your court maidens with very soft hands will do. The peasants may get my meals.
King:	Agreed. Prepare a room for the goose.
Goose:	With a hearth! And a bed covered in satin and silk.
King:	Of course.
Goose:	I deserve the very best.

Poem: I Saw a Ship A-Sailing

Act 5

Narrator: During the next months, the goose lays golden eggs each day. But the king soon grows tired of the goose's demands.

Joseph: Sire, may I present Her Royal Gooseness's "Daily List of Wants"?

Guardsman: Her Royal what?

Joseph: Her Royal Gooseness.

King: Good grief. What does she want?

Mother: Lavender soap from France.

King: Really? Feather trouble again?

Mother: Yes, Sire.

King: You don't say? And what about that beak cream? How's that working?

Mother: Not too well, Sire.

King: What a surprise.

Narrator: The king slumps in his throne.

Joseph: What's the matter, Sire?

King: I long for the old days.

Mother: Forgive us, Sire.

King: Fear not. I'm not angry with you.

Narrator: The King strokes his beard.

King: Shall we put an end to her demands?

Joseph: Just tell us what to do.

Guardsman: Sire, think of all the things you've been able to buy with those eggs!

King: But did I really need all those things? Have I even used those things? By the way, where *are* all those things?

Guardsman: Most are with the goose.

King: I see. Hmmm. Very interesting.

Mother: Sire, what are you thinking?

King: I have an idea! How many peasants live in my kingdom?

Joseph: The last count was over one hundred.

King: This castle has more than five hundred rooms. Let's spread the wealth! Tell everyone to come live here with me.

Mother: How wonderful!

Guardsman: The goose will never stand for it!

King: I know.

Guardsman: She'll want to leave.

King: Exactly. Guardsman, pack a carriage with riches, but don't forget the goose!

Narrator: Later, the king inspects the carriage. The goose is crammed into a corner. Her beak sticks out the window.

Goose: What is the meaning of this?

Narrator: The king ignores the goose.

King: Joseph, give the lead horse a thwack.

Joseph: But there's no driver, Sire. Will the horses know which direction to go?

King: It doesn't matter as long as it's far, far away.

Mother: But the horses won't know how to return.

King: That's perfectly fine. Once I was content. Then the goose came, and with her came the promise of endless riches. I became greedy. Greed is a curse. I've learned that it's better to be happy with what one has than to be miserable, always wanting more.

Narrator: Thwack! With a start, the horses and carriage charge down the pathway. As the carriage rounds the bend, all that can be heard is the loud cry of the goose.

Goose: Hoooonk!

I Saw a Ship A-Sailing

Traditional

I saw a ship a-sailing,
A-sailing on the sea.
And, oh, but it was laden
With pretty things for me.

There were comfits in the cabin,
And apples in the hold.
The sails were made of silk,
And the masts were all of gold.

The captain was a duck
With a packet on his back,
And when the ship began to move
The captain said, "Quack! Quack!"

 # April Showers
by B. G. DeSylva

Life is not a highway strewn with flowers.
Still it holds a goodly share of bliss.
When the sun gives way to April showers,
Here is the point you should never miss.
Though April showers may come your way,
They bring the flowers that bloom in May.
So if it's raining, have no regrets,
Because it isn't raining rain, you know,
It's raining violets.

Chorus:
And where you see clouds upon the hills,
You soon will see crowds of daffodils.
So keep on looking for a blue bird
And list'ning for his song
Whenever April showers come along.

Glossary

attendant—person who assists someone else

banquet—large, fancy meal for many people

carriage—vehicle in which people ride, usually pulled by horses

comfits—a type of candy

luxury—fine and expensive things

maiden—young, unmarried woman

merchant—person who runs a store or sells goods

packet—a small bundle

peasant—poor laborer

thwack—hit with the flat of the hand or a whip; the sound made by such a hit